LISA KOPPER was born in Chicago, USA and studied painting and sculpture at Carnegie-Mellon University. Lisa has illustrated more than 70 children's books, including *Daisy is a Mummy* (Dutton USA), which was shortlisted for the 1996 Kate Greenaway Medal. Her books for Frances Lincoln include *Babies' Favourites*, *Stories from the Ballet* written by Margaret Greaves and *Bring in the Holly*, written by Charles Causley.
Lisa lives in Bristol.

First published in Great Britain in 1990 by
Frances Lincoln Limited, 4 Torriano Mews,
Torriano Avenue, London NW5 2RZ
www.franceslincoln.com

First paperback edition 1994

British Library Cataloguing in Publication Data available on request

ISBN 0-7112-1702-5

Printed in Hong Kong

1 3 5 7 9 8 6 4 2

TEN
Little
Babies

**with illustrations
by Lisa Kopper**

FRANCES LINCOLN

Ten little babies sitting in a line,

one toppled over –

then there were NINE!

10

Nine greedy babies with cookies on a plate,

one ate too much –

then there were EIGHT!

9

Eight happy babies in a sandy heaven,

one lost her spade —

then there were SEVEN!

8

Seven bad babies up to naughty tricks,

one started crying —   then there were SIX!

Six speedy babies out for a lovely drive,

one lost her way —

then there were FIVE!

Five noisy babies banging on the door,

one went inside —

then there were FOUR!

5

Four dirty babies splashing with glee,

one got his hair wet —

then there were THREE!

4

Three clever babies painting red and blue,

one spilled his paints —

then there were TWO!

3

Two bouncy babies having lots of fun,

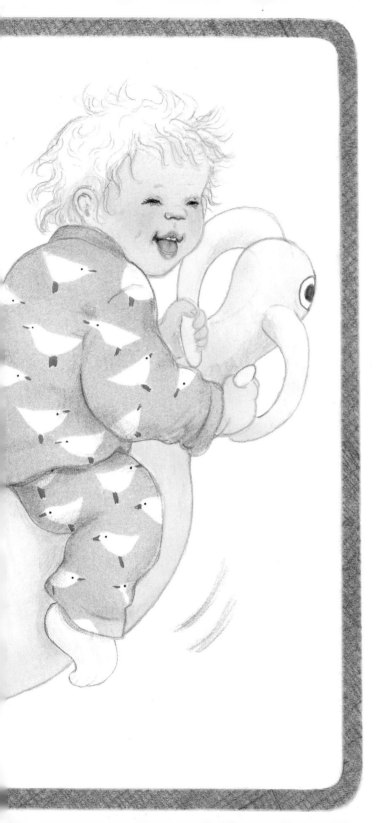

one bounced away –   then there was ONE!

2

1

One sleepy baby,
everybody's gone,

she went to sleep — then there were NONE!

MORE TITLES IN PAPERBACK
FROM FRANCES LINCOLN

BABIES' FAVOURITES

Debbie MacKinnon

Illustrated by Lisa Kopper

Toddlers will love lifting up the flaps and talking about
their favourite things in this gentle rhyming book
with lively illustrations.

ISBN 0-7112-2070-0

PEEKABOO FRIENDS

Lucy Su

Where are Robbie's friends? He looks in his boots ...
Peekaboo – he finds Giraffe! Can Robbie find
all his animal friends? Lift the flaps and see!

ISBN 0-7112-1806-4

BABIES LIKE ME

Malachy Doyle

Illustrated by Britta Teckentrup

Baby marmosets ride on their father's back
and a human baby enjoys a piggy-back from Dad.
Baby otters dive for fish and a toddler plays
and splashes with Dad in the bath. Children will
love the flaps and pop-up surprises.

ISBN 0-7112-1875-7

Frances Lincoln titles are available from all good bookshops.
You can also buy books and find out more about your favourite titles,
authors and illustrators at our website: www.franceslincoln.com.